THE

Frog Prince

A PARRAGON BOOK

Published by
Parragon Books,
Unit 13–17, Avonbridge Trading Estate,
Atlantic Road, Avonmouth, Bristol BS11 9QD

Produced by
The Templar Company plc,
Pippbrook Mill, London Road, Dorking, Surrey RH4 1JE

Designed by Mark Kingsley-Monks

Printed and bound in Italy

ISBN 0-75250-748-6

THE
Frog Prince

Retold by Caroline Repchuk
Illustrated by John James

||| •PARRAGON• |||

Once there lived a King and Queen who had three lovely daughters, but the youngest was the loveliest of all.

One hot summers' day she decided to go and play in the cool woods just outside the Palace walls.

She took with her a golden ball, her favourite toy, which she tossed high into the air and caught neatly in her little hands. She reached an open glade in the heart of the wood, and sat down by a shimmering pool of cool water.

Again she threw her ball high into the air, but this time it landed right in the middle of the pool and sank beneath the water. With a cry of dismay the Princess peered into the murky depths, but the golden ball was nowhere to be seen.

Heartbroken, the little Princess began to weep. Just then she heard a deep voice.

"Oh, Princess, why do you weep so sadly?" Startled, she looked around, but there was no one to be seen.

Then she saw a fat green frog
sitting on a lily pad nearby.
Tearfully she told him how she
had lost her golden ball.

"I can help you," replied the
frog, "but you must do
something for me in return."

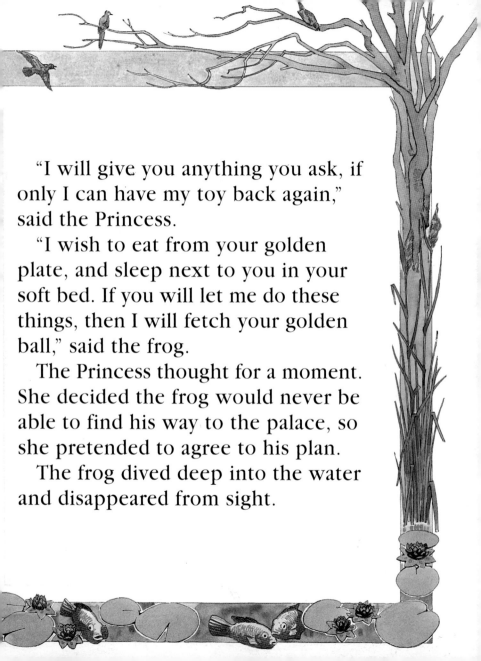

"I will give you anything you ask, if only I can have my toy back again," said the Princess.

"I wish to eat from your golden plate, and sleep next to you in your soft bed. If you will let me do these things, then I will fetch your golden ball," said the frog.

The Princess thought for a moment. She decided the frog would never be able to find his way to the palace, so she pretended to agree to his plan.

The frog dived deep into the water and disappeared from sight.

Moments later, the Princess saw a glimmer of gold as the frog swam up through the water towards her, carrying the golden ball.

Overjoyed, she grabbed the ball without even a thank-you, and ran off through the woods toward home.

By the next day she had forgotten all about the little frog. But that night as she ate dinner with her family, there was a knock at the door, and a deep voice called out:

"Open the door, Princess dear.
Open the door to your true love here.
Remember the promise that you made,
While in the cool of the greenwood
shade."

The Princess opened the
door, and there sat the wet,
slimy frog! She slammed the
door and rushed back inside.
The King saw she was upset,
and asked her what was wrong.

The Princess told her father of the promise she had made to the frog the day before, and her father looked at her sternly. "A promise is a promise,"

he said. "You must let the frog come in." The Princess reluctantly did as she was told, and the fat ugly frog hopped into the dining hall.

The frog hopped straight to
where the Princess was sitting,
and asked her to lift him up
beside her. She shivered in
disgust, but did as he asked.

"Please push your plate towards me," said the frog. "I want to share your food, just as you promised."

The little Princess glanced at her father, but he just nodded his head in answer. So she did as she was asked, and sat looking miserably at the floor while the frog ate his fill.

When he had finished, he patted his stomach and asked the Princess to carry him upstairs to bed, as he was feeling tired.

The courtiers watched with open mouths as the Princess carried the slimy frog upstairs to her lovely room.

The frog soon fell fast asleep
as he lay on the silken pillows.
The Princess vowed she would
remain awake all night, but after
a while her eyelids drooped
and she, too, fell asleep.

The next morning, before the Princess awoke, the frog hopped down from the bed, out of the door, and back to the still waters of his pond.

The Princess was relieved to find him gone when she awoke, but the next night the same thing happened all over again.

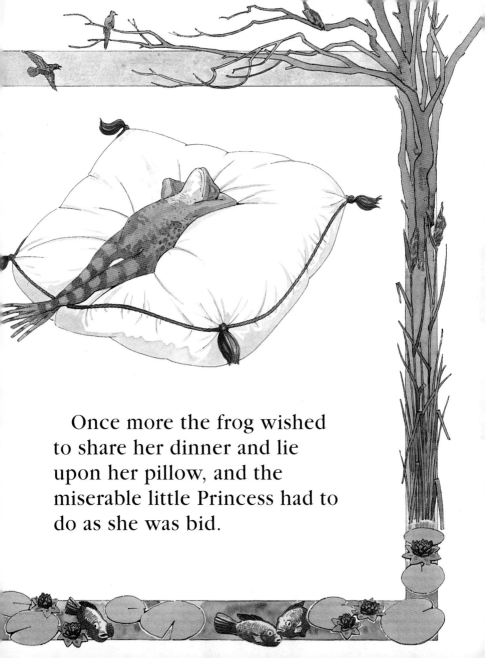

Once more the frog wished
to share her dinner and lie
upon her pillow, and the
miserable little Princess had to
do as she was bid.

The following morning he was gone
again, but he returned that evening
once more, and the poor Princess
began to think it would never end.

But when she awoke on the third
morning, she gasped to see the
handsomest Prince in the world,
standing in place of the ugly frog.

He was gazing at her tenderly.

"Sweet Princess, you have saved me from a wicked spell," he said, gently taking her hand. "An evil witch turned me into a frog and told me the only way to break the spell was to find a kind and beautiful Princess, who was willing to entertain me for three nights."

The Princess blushed to think how unwillingly she had saved the Prince. But he forgave her instantly, and falling to one knee, begged her to marry him.

And so the Prince and Princess were married, and set off for the Prince's kingdom, where they lived happily ever after.

JACOB AND WILHELM GRIMM

The German Brothers Grimm, Jacob (1785-1863)
and Wilhelm (1786-1859), gathered together over
200 old folk tales to form the classic collection of
stories now known as *Grimm's Fairy Tales.*
Before this time, *The Frog Prince* would have
been part of an oral tradition of storytelling.
Retold from generation to generation, these tales
passed on important truths about everyday life
and our fellow creatures. A child's hidden
anxieties were given shape in the form of
witches and ogres and they saw that, time and
again, the underdog would emerge victor.
These simple messages remain a valuable
contribution to each child's development
of a sense of "right" and "wrong" and help
explain why *Grimm's Fairy Tales* are so
well-loved throughout the world.